CHESHIRE MOON

Nancy Butts

FRONT STREET
ARDEN, NORTH CAROLINA
1996

For Donald and Evan,
who put up with me

Library of Congress Cataloging-in-Publication Data
Butts, Nancy   1955-
Cheshire Moon / Nancy Butts.
p.   cm.
Summary: After the death of her best friend, a twelve-year-old
hearing-impaired girl faces the choice of self-destruction through
denial and withdrawal or self-acceptance in the real, hearing world.
ISBN 1-886910-08-1 (alk. paper)
[1. Death—Fiction. 2. Self-acceptance—Fiction.
3. Deaf—Fiction. 4. Physically handicapped—Fiction.] I. Title
PZ7.B9827Ch 1996
[Fic]—dc20   95-50377

Without silence, words lose their meaning.
—Henri Nouwen, *Solitude*

CHESHIRE MOON

I

The dream came for Miranda her first night on Summerhaven.

Dreams had always haunted the island. Long before people gave it a name, Summerhaven dreamed by itself in the cold green waters of the bay.

Long before the summer people came up from Boston and Philadelphia to build their houses . . .

Long before the Micmac and the Abenaki held their clambakes on the stony beach . . .

Long before the first spruce trees sank their roots into the thin soil . . .

Even then Summerhaven wove its dreams as a spider weaves its web, spinning shadow and moonlight into mysteries that clouded the mind.

Even the gulls who plunged down to crack mussels open on the rocks were prone to dreaming. And if a gull froze in flight, dream-stunned, who could say whether the visions flickering in its head were bright—or dark?

Miranda's parents put her on the eleven o'clock ferry and waved good-bye. She did not look back. She spun around on her heel and marched up the steps to the top deck. She had it all to herself.

Miranda watched her parents shrink as the ferry pulled away from the dock, then yanked two pinkish-tan plastic molds out of her ears. She stretched her mouth in several exaggerated yawns until she felt her ears pop.

What a relief. The hearing aids didn't do any good anyway. They were supposed to help her speak. As if the garbled noise they made was any help. She couldn't hear the rumble of traffic if she stood right next to the street. How was she supposed to make sense out of the hearing aids' angry buzz?

Miranda pinched the snaillike ear molds between her fingers and dangled them overboard. All she had to do was open her fingers and— *splash!*—they would sink to the bottom of the bay. Maybe some fish could use them.

She held the hearing aids out over the rail for a moment longer, hesitating. Then slowly she drew back her arms and stuffed the tiny devices into her pockets.

Not yet. They cost a fortune. She was not ready to face her parents over this just yet.

Miranda looked back one last time at the receding shoreline. The harbor at Rockland was shrouded in fog. Her parents were swallowed up in it and quickly disappeared from view.

Miranda sat down on a wooden bench at the bow of the boat. She unwrapped the sandwich she had bought at the stand on the Rockland wharf.

Her first lobster roll of the season. It was a yearly ritual. For Miranda, the true beginning of summer was not the final bell that released her from the prison of school, but the first lobster roll on the ferry to Summerhaven.

She reached into the white paper sack and pulled out a bag of potato chips and a bottle of root beer. Timothy always drank cream soda, Miranda remembered. Suddenly the lobster roll stuck in her throat. Miranda took a swig of root beer to ease the lump down. She ate the rest of her lunch, trying not to think. The lobster roll didn't taste as good as it usually did.

The crossing to Summerhaven took two hours. Miranda stared ahead the whole time, straining to catch her first glimpse of the island.

The ferry was wrapped in a cocoon of fog. If it weren't for the wind whipping through her hair and the feel of the boat's great engines throbbing under her feet, Miranda could not have been sure that the ferry was moving.

The boat seemed stranded in the middle of the ocean, isolated in a ghostly world bounded by the slate-gray water below and a fuzzy curtain of fog just yards from the hull.

That was how she felt more and more these past several months—isolated, alone.

A black buoy materialized on the starboard side of the ferry, looming up suddenly out of the mist. It rocked back and forth in the long swells of the ferry's wake. Miranda could feel the giant gong inside the buoy the way she felt the engines thrumming in her bones.

Soon the fog turned dirty yellow. The mist parted and the fog bank rolled away in front of the boat, as if the curtains of some invisible stage were being drawn back for a performance. The sun burned through and glittered off the waves.

Up ahead Miranda spotted a low line of blue-green on the horizon. She jumped to her feet. There at last lay Summerhaven. She gathered up the remains of her lunch and tossed them in the trash.

Ten minutes later the ferry chugged into the harbor and made its way toward a concrete pier. Miranda squinted through the glare, trying to make out the small figures milling around on the shore.

The ferry had almost docked before she spotted her aunt, hanging out the window of a green pick-up truck, her dark, wiry hair tossed about in the wind. Then the truck door swung open and Aunt Kit hopped out, waving one arm wildly over her head.

Miranda waved back, and a few minutes later her aunt welcomed her with a long hug. Miranda felt the tickle of warm breath against her ear as Aunt Kit whispered something she could not hear.

Her aunt pulled back and looked Miranda full in the face. "Where are your hearing aids?" she asked, pronouncing each word with special care.

Miranda shrugged, rubbing the toe of her sneaker in the dirt.

Aunt Kit raised her eyebrows. "We're going to have a wonderful summer, I promise."

Tears stung Miranda's eyes. She touched her index finger to her lips and brought it out abruptly in a little arc in front of her. "Sure," she signed. She gave a tight smile and said nothing

Kit put one arm around Miranda's shoulders and gave her a quick squeeze. "Are you hungry? Or have you already eaten the ceremonial first lobster roll of the summer?"

Miranda snapped her thumb and middle finger in front of her mouth, her other three fingers extended. Kit looked puzzled, so Miranda patted her stomach with a look of satisfaction on her face.

"Delicious, eh?" Kit said. "Then I'll just send Mr. Leach for your bags and we'll be on our way home."

Miranda's lunch turned over in her stomach. Mr. Leach was the one who had found Timothy's empty canoe last summer. But even before that he had always made her nervous with his ancient leathery face and his crowlike black eyes.

Well, not this year, Miranda promised herself. She was twelve years old—thirteen come August— and ready for the eighth grade, no matter what her teachers said. Mr. Leach was just a gruff old man who owned a country store. Only a little kid would be afraid of him.

Mr. Leach stepped out of the truck and tipped his hat to Miranda. She ducked her head in response.

It was his truck, not Aunt Kit's. There were only three motorized vehicles on the entire island—none of them cars—and only about a half-mile of paved road. The natives walked or biked everywhere on the dirt tracks, grassy paths, and woodland trails that crisscrossed the island. Mr. Leach hired out his truck as a taxi and freight service for tourists and the summer people.

Mr. Leach swung the truck door shut behind him, then paused.

A tall, lean figure unfolded itself from the back of the pickup truck, the face in shadow from the sun dazzling directly behind it.

"I'll help," it said.

Unable to see a face, Miranda did not know what the figure had said. But for a heart-stopping second she thought it was Timothy.

It can't be, she told herself, and then a boy stepped out of the shadows and her heart started beating normally again.

Of course it wasn't Timothy. This boy was taller, thin-faced, with a tan that probably came from year-round work outdoors and not just summer fun. He had dark reddish-brown hair too, not Timothy's sandy blond.

"Thanks, Boone," Kit said. Glancing at her niece, she added, "Miranda, this is Boone Ligonier." Awkwardly Kit began to bend her fingers in a series of different shapes. She gave up abruptly with a shake of her head.

Miranda, eyebrows lifted in a question, looked

at her aunt. She sketched a circle in front of her mouth with one finger, then pointed to the boy.

"I was trying to tell you his name, but I have never been any good at fingerspelling. Boone," Kit said, mouthing the word distinctly. "He helps me out around the house and studio."

Was she saying "moon" or "Boone," Miranda wondered. M and B look a lot alike when you are trying to read lips.

"Boone, this is my niece, Miranda Cooper."

The boy grabbed Miranda's hand and shook it with a firm grip. "Hi."

Miranda pulled her hand away.

The only person who had ever shaken Miranda's hand was the school psychologist, Dr. Stein. Dr. Frankenstein, Miranda called him, because he spent all those Thursday afternoons trying to tame the stubborn monster everyone thought Miranda had become. "Everyone" being her parents and the principal and her teacher, Mrs. Davenport. Miranda didn't like Dr. Stein one bit.

"Come on, hop in the truck and let's get you out of this wind," Kit said, giving Miranda a little push with one hand. "Your hair's damp, and your cheeks feel frozen."

Miranda climbed into the cab of the truck. She hadn't been watching her aunt's face, so she had no idea what Kit had just said. Her eyes followed Boone as he disappeared onto the ferry.

She hoped he wasn't going to spend too much time hanging around Aunt Kit's house. She didn't have the patience to break in another hearing kid. This summer, she just wanted to be left alone.

Boone hustled off to the ferry to help with Miranda's bags. Mr. Leach was struggling to lift two enormous suitcases.

"Here, let me take one of those," Boone offered.

"Feels like the girl is moving here permanent," Mr. Leach grumbled.

"Is she mute, too?" Boone asked, huffing a little as he shouldered his load. "I mean, Kit—"

Mr. Leach glared at him.

"*Miss* Cooper, that is," Boone corrected. "She told me her niece was deaf, but . . ." His voice dropped. "Can't she talk either?"

"Ayuh, the girl can talk," Mr. Leach replied. "At least she could when I saw her last."

Neither one spoke while they trudged off the ferry and back onto the wharf. Mr. Leach added, "Maybe the girl's just got nothing to say."

Twelve hours later, after a hot bath and a supper of clam chowder, Miranda climbed into the big iron bed under the window and watched the stars. A light breeze carried the woodsy smell of pine and damp earth into the room, along with the faint coppery tang of the sea. The Great Square of Pegasus wheeled through the branches of the old oak tree, the clock of stars telling her it was well past midnight.

It had been a long day.

Miranda's eyelids drooped as she slowly tumbled into sleep. There, under the spinning stars in the big iron bedstead, the dream came for her.

And in his narrow bed in an attic two miles away, the dream came for Boone too.

II

Miranda's hands danced in her sleep, fingers fluttering over the faded scrapwork quilt like a flight of birds.

Time and again her hand flew to her face. Two fingers, shaped in a V, pointed to her eyes, and swung around into the shadowy stillness of the bedroom. Then they dove down and touched the center of her chest. "Look in."

Miranda's head tossed back and forth on her pillow, but she did not wake up. Her hands continued their silent ballet.

At last she swept her arms up into the fading darkness, straining to grasp something just out of reach. Then they fell back to the quilt, and were still.

She awoke, and the dream drifted off like a wisp of smoke.

Miranda squeezed her eyes shut and tried to stay asleep. If she hurried, maybe she could get back to the dream before it slipped away.

But it was already too late. Even now she was forgetting. The things that had seemed so real while she was dreaming them, so wonderful, were fading back into the shadows.

Like the tidal pool where she and her cousin Timothy used to swim. In the dream she was waiting there, standing at the ledge high in the rocks where a pool of water was trapped between the tides. She knelt down and the tide rushed in, swift and deep, swirling her nightgown behind her.

Even though she was tucked in her bed, the dream seemed as vivid to Miranda as if she had actually been standing on the rocks just a while ago. She shivered. She could almost feel the water chilling her bare feet.

There was something else—something important. But what? Something about fireflies, and the moon, and a storm of light over the ocean. Something about Timothy?

The dream trembled at the edge of her memory for one last moment, then vanished completely.

Miranda sprang up from her pillow, clutching the sheet between her fingers. She glanced around the room, searching the familiar corners, then shook her head. What did she expect to find? It was the same old bedroom she slept in every summer.

Lace curtains screened the window. Her jeans and T-shirt lay in a heap on the rag rug where she had dumped them last night. The whitewashed board walls were bare except for a small mirror in the shape of a ship's wheel and a blue and yellow print of the moon.

Miranda let out a breath. She felt a tightness in her chest. The dream had left a bittersweet feeling behind. A feeling like the day after Christmas when all the presents are unwrapped and it is time to take down the tree. Like she had lost something—or someone.

Her cousin Timothy. She had lost him forever, swept out to sea last September in a battered green canoe. They would never share the summers here at their Aunt Kit's house again.

Miranda blinked hard. She bit her lip and threw off the covers. If only she could remember more of the dream! She wondered whether it was worth trying to fall asleep again.

Sleeping was better than being awake anyway. When she was asleep, she didn't have to miss Timothy so much. She didn't have to think about being held back in school next year. And she didn't have to feel alone all the time.

A gray square of dawn showed through the window. Miranda swung her legs over the edge of the bed. She was wide awake. It was too late now to go back to sleep. She steeled herself to face another endless day.

As her feet hit the wood-planked floor, the bottom of her nightgown brushed against her ankles. The hem was damp.

Boone catapulted upright, instantly awake. His heart pounded, and the Celtics T-shirt he wore to bed was plastered to his body with sweat.

Ricocheting over and over again in his mind were the words "Look in."

"What the heck does that mean?" Boone said to

himself.

He grabbed the pad of drawing paper he kept on the crate by his bed. Boone's hand danced across the page and sketchy images began to form: a cloud of fireflies on the lawn, the silver crescent of the moon hanging like a giant grin in the sky, and a storm of light beating down on the waves off Summerhaven. It was all he could remember—bits and pieces of the dream, odd fragments that made no sense.

Nothing to make his heart hammer so hard in his chest.

Boone stared down at the pad. He sat with his head in his hands for a moment, then shrugged it off. After all, it was just a dream.

His mother yelled at him from the yard outside. "Boone! Boone, get up, you hear me? I'm late already."

He glanced at the clock. It was nearly five. The sun was up, and his mother was on her way to catch the first ferry to the mainland. She would spend the next three days there working twelve-hour shifts as a nurse. She stayed over at the hospital in Rockland and would not return until Sunday evening. Boone was in charge of his younger brothers and sisters until then. Grampa didn't get around so well since he broke his hip, and Granma wasn't much help either. Her thinking was all muddled.

Boone got out of bed. He pushed open a window beside the bricks of the chimney that rose through his attic bedroom. "G'morning, Mom."

"Grampa needs help with his bath today, and don't forget our grass wants cutting before you go running off to that painter woman's."

"She's an *artist*, Mom. She lets me hang around her studio and watch sometimes, and she teaches me stuff."

"Yeah, well, she should get a real job, see what it feels like to break her back for a living."

Boone sighed. "She pays me for the work I do."

His mother hoisted a large bag over her shoulder. "That counts for something, I guess. I'm late, I gotta go."

"Don't worry about anything, Mom," Boone said. "I'll take care of stuff."

In Portsmouth he would have added, "I'll miss you, Mom." But that was before his dad left and they had to move back to the island and take care of his grandparents. Now his mother was so grouchy all the time that he was glad to see her go. He felt bad about that.

Just then Mr. Leach's green truck rattled up into the yard, and his mom got in.

Shivering a little in the cool morning air, Boone shut the window. He threw on a pair of jeans and a clean T-shirt, then began stripping the sheets and blanket off his bed. Friday was the day he changed the linens in the house and did the laundry.

As he reached down to pull up the fitted sheet at the bottom of his bed, crushed shells scattered across the floor.

Boone frowned. He bundled up the dirty sheets

and headed down the attic stairs. He'd sweep up the shells later. He had too much other work to do now.

III

"**D**id you sleep all right?"

Aunt Kit bounded around the kitchen, her face powdered with flour. Flecks of yellow batter speckled her hair.

Miranda rubbed her eyes and shrugged.

"I thought I heard you on the stairs in the middle of the night," Kit said, attacking a bowl of batter with a wooden spoon. "I wondered if you'd come down to make yourself a tuna sandwich or something."

Miranda touched her chest and shook her head. "Not me," she signed. She had been upstairs in bed all night long, dreaming.

Kit poured a cup of blueberries into the bowl. "I thought you might like pancakes this morning—a special treat for your first day back on Summerhaven. Just don't get used to it. It will be cornflakes for breakfast most days around here. I like to catch the early light."

Miranda watched her aunt's face intently while she spoke, struggling to follow the movements of her mouth and piece together what she was saying. It was hard. Was her aunt saying something about pancakes—or maybe bandaids?

Bandaids didn't make sense, Miranda figured. With that bowlful of batter in her arms, Aunt Kit must be talking about pancakes.

"So are pancakes okay with you?" Kit asked.

Miranda balled her right hand into a fist and bobbed it up and down twice. "Yes," she signed.

"Good." Kit turned to the ancient black cookstove that took up a whole corner of the kitchen. She struck a match and lit one of the stove's six cast-iron burners.

Miranda poured herself a glass of orange juice and sipped it.

"Looks like it's going to be another spectacular day," Kit said. "Not a cloud in the sky. Though I hope we get some rain soon. We haven't had a drop in days."

Miranda plunked her glass down, spilling a few drops of juice on the table.

It *must* have rained last night—rain came in through the open window beside her bed. How else could the hem of her nightgown have gotten wet? Miranda curved both hands into claws and dropped them down twice from shoulder to chest level. She finished with two more quick gestures.

"I don't sign as well as Timothy did," Aunt Kit said.

Miranda sucked in her breath. She felt as if someone had just punched her in the stomach.

"All I caught was the word 'rain' there at the start," her aunt went on, not noticing. "I don't get enough practice, I guess. You're going to have to tell me in words, not signs."

Miranda scowled, bringing her thumb and first two fingers together like an alligator snapping its jaws shut. "No!" she signed. Her whole arm shook.

Aunt Kit turned the flame down under the griddle. "Your dad told me that you weren't talking anymore."

Still frowning, Miranda gestured rapidly, hands and arms slicing through the air like knives.

"I can't follow that, Miranda. You're going too fast."

Miranda slapped the heel of her right hand down twice across her upturned left palm.

"What's that?" Kit asked.

Miranda impatiently repeated the gesture, then made a scribbling motion across her palm.

"Oh, I get it. Yes, I've got some paper somewhere." Kit rummaged through a series of drawers before she came up with a small pad and a pencil stub. "Here."

Miranda wrote quickly, then handed the pad to her aunt.

"Do talk—with signs, not voice," she had written. The word "do" was underlined three times.

"I think you know what your father meant, Miranda. He said it was causing you problems at school. You won't talk to your teachers or classmates, and they don't understand sign language."

Miranda grabbed the pad of paper back from her aunt and scribbled furiously.

Kit stood behind her and looked over her shoulder.

"Why speak?" Miranda had scrawled. "Nobody uses my language—not teachers, doctor. Not Mother and Daddy."

Miranda slammed the pad down on the kitchen table.

Kit wheeled around in front of Miranda and crouched so Miranda could see her face. "I know it's not easy. But can you really expect the rest of the world to learn to sign, just for you?"

Miranda glanced at her aunt for a moment, then wrote two words on the paper. She showed Kit. "Timothy learned."

Miranda stared down at the table. On Summerhaven, she and Timothy had made their own world. A world where it didn't matter whether you spoke with your hands or your lips. Sometimes she even forgot that he was hearing and she was deaf. They just let their hands take off, and they understood each other completely.

Kit turned to the stove and flipped the pancakes, then swung around to face Miranda again. "He was my nephew as well as your cousin," she said. "I miss him too. Every day."

They were both still for a long moment.

"Dreamed Timothy last night," Miranda scribbled on her pad.

Kit waited for Miranda to go on. When she didn't, Kit asked, "Do you want to talk about it?"

Miranda moved both fists forward through the air as if she were trying to push something.

"Trying, but can't remember. Sky falling, but not scary . . ."

Miranda's writing trailed off. She pinched her fingers shut and touched them to her mouth, then spread them apart as she traced a circle in the air around her face.

"Beautiful," she wrote.

Kit smiled.

"Didn't want to wake up." Miranda's shoulders sagged, and she put down the pencil.

"Did it make you feel sad?" Kit asked.

Miranda shook her head. "No!" she signed. She raked her fingers down her face. "Mad!" she wrote in big letters.

Kit came over and sat next to her, pulling Miranda's head against her shoulder. She stroked her hair, and rocked her slightly, as if she were much younger than twelve.

Suddenly Kit's nose twitched. "Ohmigosh," she exclaimed. "My pancakes are burning." She rushed to the stove and snatched the griddle off the flame, then dumped the pancakes on two blue china plates and carried them to the table. "Dig in."

But just as Miranda was twirling her scorched pancakes through a lake of maple syrup, Mr. Leach tapped at the window.

"Door's open," Kit called.

Mr. Leach walked into the kitchen and tipped his hat.

"Good morning, Mr. Leach," Kit said. "You're welcome to pancakes if you're hungry. Blueberry."

"No thank you, miss, I've already had my mug up this morning. Anyway, I can't stay. I just brought along your mail." He handed Kit a pile of envelopes.

"And a message," Mr. Leach continued. "A call came in for you this morning over at the store. It was your brother, asking after the young lady here."

He tilted his head toward where Miranda sat and gave her a sideways glance. She looked away.

"I told him she made the crossing in one piece. You're welcome to return the call at the store, but mind you, I close sharp at five." He lifted his hat again and turned to go. "I'll be on my way now."

He stopped and stared at Miranda before he got to the door.

"Cheshire moon last night," he said.

Miranda wrinkled her forehead. Was he saying something about the moon? Or was he talking about that boy Boone from the dock yesterday?

"I saw it," Kit said. "It always reminds me of the Cheshire Cat in *Alice in Wonderland*."

"Same smile, same mysterious ways." Mr. Leach said. "You watch tonight and see for yourself."

He twisted the knob on the back door and looked right at Miranda. "Folks get some pretty strange dreams hereabouts when the moon smiles."

Miranda gulped down a swallow of orange juice. Her throat had just gone dry.

IV

Miranda rinsed the last of the breakfast dishes in the big soapstone sink, set the griddle in the rack to dry, and turned off the faucet. She hated washing dishes, but there was nothing better to do. The day stretched out ahead of her, too many long, empty hours to fill before she could go to bed again.

The days had never been long enough when Timothy was alive. "Let's go exploring," he would say, and they would traipse off through the woods or poke around the cobwebby corners of the attic. They climbed apple trees in Aunt Kit's orchard or canoed around Frenchman's Cove, played backgammon on the front porch, or rode their bicycles down to the village for ice cream cones.

But today, the first day of her first summer without Timothy, Miranda could think of nothing she wanted to do. With a sigh, she tucked the pad and pencil in the pocket of her jeans and began to prowl through the rooms of the house.

She climbed a narrow flight of stairs to the second floor and hesitated outside Timothy's old room. She took a deep breath and stepped inside.

A bed, a desk, a chest of drawers. Books lined a shelf over the desk and a telescope—one that she and Timothy had made together by hand—stood in the corner.

The air smelled stale. Even if she closed her eyes and tried to pretend that Timothy had just gone down to the kitchen for a glass of milk, Miranda could sense that he wasn't there anymore. The room felt hollow, drained of life.

She went over to the window seat and peered down at her aunt's studio in the back yard. Through the skylight in the studio roof, she could see Aunt Kit squeezing tubes of paint on a wooden board.

Then Aunt Kit turned her head back over her shoulder and mouthed something to someone. Miranda looked in the same direction and saw the lanky, dark-haired boy who had shaken her hand at the dock yesterday. Mr. Moon-Boone.

What's he doing here? Miranda jerked her head inside the window like a turtle withdrawing into its shell. She didn't want him to see her and hoped Aunt Kit didn't have the bright idea that Miranda and what's-his-name should hang around together. Miranda's parents were always doing things like that—trying to make friends for her. She hated it.

Miranda slid off the window seat and turned to face the room. Its emptiness echoed inside her. Suddenly she had to get outside. She took the stairs two at a time and headed out through long grass and orange hawkweed to the woods.

Her feet led her over a path through spruce and fir trees. Ferns covered the ground like giant green feathers, dotted with the white flowers of bunchberry. The path ran downhill, stopping short at the edge of a steep earthen bank. Tree roots bulged out of the thin springy earth. Twenty feet below, the waters of Frenchman's Cove lapped against the rocks.

Miranda paused. Of all the places she and Timothy had loved, this was the best. They had sat here by the hour watching the tides rise and fall, watching the clouds pile high in the afternoon sky and change the seascape from gray to green to blue.

A ladderlike wooden stairway led down the bluff to the cove. Miranda descended the steps to the water's edge.

The tide was going out. A mud flat glistened across half the cove. Seaweed lay limp on exposed rocks. Miranda wrinkled her nose at the rank smell of mud and rotten vegetation baking in the sun. She stepped cautiously across the slippery rocks to where a cherry-red canoe was beached in the soft green muck.

Miranda's throat tightened. Aunt Kit had bought a new canoe. She wondered what Aunt Kit had done with the old one, the beat-up green boat that Mr. Leach had found washed up on a beach down-island.

Miranda squatted and began untying the line that moored the canoe to a hemlock tree back on the bank. She had been struggling with the stubborn knot for a long time when a stone splashed into the water beside her.

Miranda whipped around.

Boone—that must be his name. Nobody is called Moon—stood on the rocky beach about ten yards away. He was waving and moving his mouth rapidly. Miranda had trouble making out what he was saying.

She chopped her right hand against the palm of her left.

His mouth kept moving.

Miranda dropped the boat line and slogged back through the mud to the foot of the bluff. She made the chopping motion again, then dragged the fingers of her right hand slowly down the back of her left hand from fingertips to wrist.

He didn't get it. Miranda clenched her fists until the bones showed white beneath the skin. If he didn't slow down she would never be able to understand him.

She decided to ignore him. She plopped down on a tree root, picked up a stick, and began to scrape the mud off her sneakers. When she was done, she wiped the mud off her hands on a patch of moss and dried them on her jeans. Only then did she look up at him.

Boone's mouth was still moving. He was saying something about Aunt Kit that Miranda couldn't understand.

Miranda scowled. She tugged on Boone's hand and motioned for him to crouch down beside her. Then she grabbed his chin, shifting his face until it was so close to her own that she could see the gold flecks in his cloudy green eyes.

"What's the matter?" Boone asked.

Miranda pointed to her eyes, then pointed to Boone's mouth and shook her head.

"Oh, sorry." Boone flushed. "You need to see my face better, huh? I was saying that I was just up at your aunt's. I work for her, odd jobs mostly, but she lets me hang around her studio sometimes and watch her."

Miranda brushed the first two fingers of her right hand across the open palm of her left, then pointed to Boone.

Boone shook his head, a puzzled look on his face. "I don't understand."

Miranda dug down in her pocket and pulled out a pencil and paper. "You paint?" She printed each word in capital letters, slowly, as if she were writing to a first grader who was just learning to spell.

"I try." Boone laughed. "I thought I was pretty good too, until I saw what Kit can do. But she's teaching me." He paused. "Show me again how you say 'paint' in sign language."

Miranda sighed. She knew she'd get stuck with him. Impatiently she repeated the brushing gesture.

Boone tried it himself, and a grin lit up his thin face. "That's like charades—it sort of looks like you're painting. Are all signs that way?"

Miranda shook her head.

Boone fell silent. At last he said, as if in apology, "You're pretty good at reading lips."

"Speechreading," Miranda wrote, pressing the

pencil hard into the paper. She tore off the top sheet. The grooves of the letters showed through on the blank paper below.

"Why are you so mad?" Boone asked.

Miranda glared at him.

"I'm sorry I don't understand sign language, but you read lips. What's keeping you from talking to me?"

Miranda's eyes flashed. "Nothing," she wrote. "I can talk."

"Then why don't you?"

Miranda bent her head and fiddled with her shoelace. When she looked up at Boone again she shrugged.

"Oh-kay," Boone said, stretching out the syllables of the word. "We sure got off on the wrong foot."

They both stared out at the waves for a long time, not looking at each other.

Suddenly Miranda began to write fast. She tore off the page and thrust it at Boone, studying his face while he read.

"Talking doesn't make you smart. I'm good at math and computers—I'm deaf, not stupid. But teachers want to hold me back because I sign, not talk."

"What about the other deaf kids?" Boone asked. "Do they get held back for signing, too?"

"No others," Miranda wrote.

Boone shook his head. "That must be tough—to be the only one. And to get held back when you can do the work. Grownups can be pretty dense sometimes," he said. "Maybe they'll change their minds."

Miranda rolled her eyes. Not unless she started talking again. And she had no intention of doing that.

"Say, how old are you, anyway?" Boone asked. "I'm almost fourteen. Going into ninth grade."

Miranda turned her palm inward and held out her thumb and first two fingers. She wiggled her fingers twice, then scratched "13" on the pad of paper. "In August," she added, after a moment's pause.

"Can you show me how to do fourteen?" Boone asked.

Miranda wiggled the four fingers of her right hand in toward her body a couple of times.

Boone turned his hand around and waved at himself. Miranda reached over and folded his thumb against his palm, and he repeated the hand-waving action. This time she nodded.

"Maybe you can teach me more sometime."

Miranda did not reply. Sometimes hearing kids were interested in signing for a while, but it never lasted long. They learned a few signs like "toilet" and "vomit" that made them giggle, then used them to goof around in class behind the teacher's back. They never learned enough to talk to her.

Miranda turned her face away and rose to her feet. She was tired of writing notes, tired of struggling to follow the movements of Boone's lips and piece together what he was saying. It had been so much easier with Timothy.

She looked out over the cove. She had spent many hours here with Timothy, digging for mussels at low tide, paddling around in the canoe when the water was calm.

But the water had changed on Timothy that day, a squall line tearing through and sucking his canoe out of the cove. His body had never been found.

He was still out there somewhere.

Boone stepped in front of Miranda and bent his head so she could see his face. "What's wrong?"

Miranda turned away and stomped up the stairs, the wood shaking with every step.

V

As the sun slipped below the horizon, the first stars kindled in the east. The sky over the bay turned cobalt blue, like the milk of magnesia bottles Mr. Leach stocked high on the back shelves of his store. The blue rapidly deepened to black, until the line where the water ended and the sky began disappeared.

Miranda stretched out on her bed and propped her arms and chin on the windowsill. Mingled with the familiar smells of salt and pine and sun-baked earth, the sweet fragrance of woodsmoke hung in the air. Someone was having a campfire. Miranda breathed in the scent of smoke and remembered.

On her birthday each August she and Timothy packed up their sleeping bags and telescope and camped out in the meadow to count shooting stars. They blistered their tongues eating hot dogs straight from the sticks they were roasted on, and licked gooey marshmallows off their fingers.

Then Miranda lay back while Timothy pointed out stars, planets, nebulae, and the craters of the moon. She'd look through the telescope, then watch in the dancing firelight as Timothy signed the names of what she'd seen.

"There's Pegasus, the Winged Horse." He looked silly wiggling his fingers on the side of his head like horse's ears, then brushing his fingertips off his shoulders in the sign for wings. "It's my favorite constellation."

"And there's the Milky Way." He swept his hand across the sky, tracing the path of a great cloud of stars. "The Indians believed that the souls of the dead cross over it on their final journey home."

Miranda grimaced at the memory. Nobody paddled across a river of stars any more than they put on wings and halos or spooked people in creepy old houses. Another worthless folktale. It sounded pretty, but it wasn't true. Just like stories about ghosts or angels—or Mr. Leach's Cheshire moon.

The moon. What was it Mr. Leach had said about strange dreams?

Miranda sat up and pressed her face against the screen to look out the window, but it was no use. She couldn't see the moon from here. Her bedroom faced east. The new moon, only two days old, was in the west, trailing the sunset.

Miranda crossed the hall to Timothy's room and crouched in the window seat. She searched the dark patches of sky that were visible between the trees. At last she spotted a hook-shaped glimmer hanging low in the sky.

There behind a leafy birch gleamed the Cheshire moon.

A draft of air whispered against the back of her

neck, and Miranda shivered. The moon did look like a huge, faceless grin. No wonder Mr. Leach said people had strange dreams.

Miranda tucked her nightgown around her ankles. Forget about Mr. Leach's stupid old haunted moon. It didn't matter what kind of dreams it conjured up. No dream could bring Timothy back.

Miranda walked over to the telescope and drew a circle in the blanket of dust which covered it. She felt as dark and empty as Timothy's deserted room.

Dead was dead. No tall tale could change that. When somebody died, all they left behind was an ever-fading memory.

Miranda bit her lip and hurried across the hall to bed. She wanted to get back to the dream. She wriggled down under the quilt and squinched her eyes shut. But the more she tried to fall asleep, the more wide awake she became. So she watched the stars parade in the open stretch of sky over the bay, and as she watched she remembered Timothy. Timothy signing in the firelight, Timothy peering through his telescope. She wanted never to forget.

At last she slept—and began to dream.

Miranda fled into the woods along a green trail of light, then found herself alone on a narrow spit of land surrounded by the sea. Black waves moved restlessly against the rocks. A small island stood offshore.

Miranda looked up, and the sky fell in a hailstorm of light.

The last thing she saw as the dream faded was a

dark figure standing on the wave-tossed island. She reached out her arms to sign, but her hands were strange and clumsy. The signs died on her fingertips. She awoke with tears on her face.

Boone didn't have time to notice the sunset.

He sliced hot dogs into a pan of baked beans and slid them into the oven. He wiped up the same beans an hour later after Nicky, the youngest, gave his plate to the dog, who vomited all over the kitchen floor.

"Claudia, get Nicky in his pajamas and put him to bed," Boone said, wringing a dirty sponge into a bucket of water.

"Do I have to?" Claudia whined.

"Would you rather do this?" Boone waved the sponge in her face.

"Come on, Nicky," Claudia said, scooping the little boy out of his chair and hoisting him on her hip.

Boone carried the bucket to the sink and dumped the water down the drain. "Suzanne, it's your turn to do the dishes."

"What about Jeremy?" Suzanne said, piling knives and forks onto plates with a loud clatter. "Doesn't he have to do anything?"

"I asked him to take Grampa to the bathroom."

"Well, don't hold your breath," Boone's sister said. "I think Jeremy left ten minutes ago to play ball down at the church."

Boone dropped the bucket. "Oh, no," he groaned,

rushing out of the kitchen toward his grandparents' room. "I just gave him a bath this morning. Jeremy's going to catch it if I have to do it again."

He did have to bathe Grampa again, and change his sheets. By the time Boone yelled at his brother, got everyone to bed, and finally escaped to the attic, the narrow sliver of moon had long since set.

Boone sagged down on his bed and stared at the poster of van Gogh's *Starry Night* tacked to the bare rafters in the ceiling.

Why did he have to take care of everybody? Things had been different last year, back in Portsmouth. Not good, maybe, but better than this.

Here it was summer, school was out, and Boone didn't even have time to knock around a few balls with the guys after supper. Who was he kidding? He hadn't even had time to make any real friends here on the island.

He wondered where Pop was now.

"This is *your* job," he called out loud. He stripped off his jeans and snatched at the string dangling from the light bulb overhead, yanking it so hard that it snapped off. The room was plunged in darkness.

Great. Something else he would have to fix tomorrow.

Boone lay on top of the covers, wide-eyed and stiff, one arm behind his head. It was a long time before he fell asleep. But when he slept, he dreamed.

Panting, Boone chased a swarm of fireflies through the woods. Though he pumped his legs hard, he could not keep up. The blinking green line of light snaked far ahead of him. Tree branches lashed his arms, and ferns tangled in his feet.

He fought to keep pace, his heart drumming in his chest with the need to *get there, get there, hurry.* But when he finally burst out of the woods onto the stony beach, he had no idea where he was. He did not recognize the island rising out of the waves.

Then the light pounded down on him, and he saw the deaf girl, Miranda, riding a canoe across the choppy water.

VI

The dream retreated to its web of darkness, stranding Miranda and Boone abruptly in the shallows of sleep. In their bedrooms two miles apart, they both awakened at the same time.

Miranda flopped over on her stomach, buried her head under her pillow, and fell back into a fitful sleep.

Boone opened one eye and glanced over at the clock. Four A.M. and the sky was already turning gray. Dawn crept up early on the island in summer.

Boone rubbed his hands over his face. Two nightmares in a row. He hadn't slept this badly since Pop walked out.

But the dreams were not about his father. He wasn't sure what they were about, except that Miranda Cooper had turned up in the last one.

Boone reached for his drawing pad, flipped back yesterday's page with the sketch of the meteor shower on it, and started a new picture. His hand slid slowly across the paper, stopping for long periods while he closed his eyes and tried to bring back what he had seen in the dream. He started over several times, ripping off each aborted effort and piling it on the floor beside the bed.

Boone tore off the final page and examined it with a small frown. He had sketched the image of an island, little more than a pile of rock crowned with a spiky row of trees.

So what? There were hundreds of nameless islands scattered across Penobscot Bay. Boone didn't recognize this one. He couldn't see why dreaming about it should bother him so.

He caught sight of the clock: 6:17! He'd been drawing for over two hours.

It was crazy to waste this much time worrying about a dream—he was late, and he had a lot of work to do. Boone leapt out of bed, swiftly tucking in the sheets and blankets and scooping the pile of sketch paper off the floor.

He fixed a pot of oatmeal for his brothers and sisters, boiled two eggs for his grandparents, then biked over to cut the long grass in Kit's orchard.

The scent of fresh-cut grass greeted Miranda when she finally got up. She had dozed uneasily in her bed until the morning sun streamed through her window.

Miranda shaded her eyes. She felt that same bittersweet day-after-Christmas mood again this morning.

She kicked off the covers and got dressed. Heading down the stairs for breakfast, she slipped on something rubbery and slick. She bent down and discovered a hazel-brown strand of rockweed. It was still wet. Miranda fingered it, wondering who had tracked it inside.

She picked up the slimy rockweed and stepped down to the hall. At the foot of the staircase, near the front door, a small patch of water glistened on the floor.

Maybe Aunt Kit went for an early morning walk down at Frenchman's Cove, Miranda thought as she fixed juice and cinnamon toast. When she had swallowed her last mouthful, she decided to check the puddle again. It had dried up almost completely, leaving a faint white film of salt behind.

Miranda washed her plate and glass and went out back to the studio. Aunt Kit was glowering at a large canvas and rubbing paint off one corner with a rag. Miranda walked up to her and tapped her on the shoulder.

Aunt Kit turned around to face Miranda and smiled. "Good morning."

Miranda patted her pockets and fished out the pad and pencil, still stowed there from yesterday. "You walked at cove today?" she wrote.

"No," her aunt said. She raised her eyebrows. "Why do you ask?"

"Never mind," Miranda scribbled.

Kit stuffed the paint-smeared rag in one of the pockets in her white overalls. "Did you have another dream last night?"

Miranda looked away—down at the floor, at the canvases stacked against the walls, everywhere but at Aunt Kit. She didn't want to talk about the dreams with anybody.

Aunt Kit grasped Miranda's chin and turned her face so they could see each other clearly. "The first time I came to Summerhaven, I had the most remarkable dream." She paused. "It was a Cheshire moon then, too. Never had one since, but I wondered . . ."

Miranda moved back a step.

"Well, you've seemed a bit . . . distracted the past two mornings." Aunt Kit looked at her closely. "And you mentioned that dream about Timothy yesterday."

"No," Miranda wrote. "No more dreams."

Kit unscrewed a tube and squeezed a scarlet ribbon of paint onto a wooden board. "Then on with business. I wanted to ask if you could help out today."

Miranda spelled out the letters O and K with her fingers.

"Boone's about finished mowing the orchard. I've asked him to tackle the garden afterward. It's overgrown with weeds, and the old rock wall along the back needs to be rebuilt. It's a tough job—even with two of you, it could take all summer to finish."

Miranda tried not to let her feelings show in her face. She didn't mind the work, but she wasn't so sure about being thrown together with Boone again.

Miranda dragged herself over to the apple orchard. She tucked a few stray hairs into her ponytail and wiped her palms on her jeans. Maybe they'd get along better today.

Boone was mowing around the last apple tree, a Red Sox baseball cap perched backward on his head. The orchard was now crisscrossed with neat, grassy paths like a tic-tac-toe game. A wiry old tree stood in the center of each square.

Boone pushed the mower to the side of the orchard and switched it off. He pulled a blue bandanna out of his jeans pocket and mopped sweat from his forehead.

Miranda walked up, positioning herself directly in front of him.

His mouth tightened in a thin line. "I know Kit sent you down here, but I don't need your help."

Miranda studied the expression on Boone's face. She understood what he had said, but she wasn't sure what he meant. Was he trying to let her off the hook because he thought she couldn't do the work? The words he had mouthed said one thing, the grim line of his lips said another.

She clenched her hands into fists and shook them once in the air, at chest level.

"What?" Boone asked.

Miranda took out her pad of paper. "I'm strong," she wrote.

"Fine." Boone tucked the bandanna back in his pocket. "Let's start with the garden first. You should be able to handle that."

"Fine," Miranda wrote. Then she spread out the fingers of her right hand, and placed her thumb in the center of her chest. She tapped the word "fine" on the paper and repeated the sign.

"Look, if you can't be bothered to talk to me, I don't see why I should bother to learn your stupid signs."

Miranda's mouth dropped open. She snapped it shut and marched over to the garden. She dropped to her knees. What . . . an . . . *idiot*, she thought, yanking out a weed for each word.

Boone squatted down next to Miranda and tapped her on the shoulder.

She jerked away and kept weeding.

Boone pivoted around in front of her. Miranda refused to look up until he clamped his hand on her wrist. "Look, I'm sorry."

Miranda glared at him.

"That was a bonehead thing to say."

Miranda's expression did not change. She snatched her pad out of her pocket and wrote, "Just keep working."

Boone stood up and stalked over to a dilapidated red barn. He came back a few moments later with two hoes, handing one to Miranda.

The two worked side by side without signing or talking or passing notes. When Miranda sneaked a glance over at Boone, he was attacking the ground with his hoe as if he were at war with it.

What right did *he* have to be angry?

When they finished chopping weeds in the rows of newly sprouted corn and lettuce and peas, they started on the old rock wall, not even stopping for something to drink.

And still they did not talk.

As the sun climbed high in the cloudless blue sky, the air grew hot and still. Miranda twisted her ponytail into a loose knot to keep the hair off her neck. Boone took off his shirt.

Fixing the wall was hard work. They had to pry up the rocks with their fingers, digging out vines and weeds and decades of matted dirt to loosen the stones. Then they either brushed off the stone and set it back in place, or hauled in a new stone from a pile of rocks cleared from the garden earlier that spring.

As they worked, they evicted creatures from their homes in the wall. Miranda gave a strangled shriek when a large black beetle scuttled up her arm after she'd dislodged a rock.

Boone whipped around, his hoe raised like an ax. "So, you can scream," he said. "I thought it was a copperhead from the fuss you were making."

After that, Miranda kept a close watch for bugs and spiders and mice—and snakes.

The sun peaked overhead, then began its slow slide back down the sky. Miranda's muscles ached with the strain of all the bending and stooping and carrying. Her fingers were scraped and bloody. She dropped on the ground, leaned back against the still-unfinished wall, and closed her eyes.

A few seconds later she felt vibrations against her back and thighs, and she knew that Boone had sat down too.

Something stung the side of her neck. Miranda

opened her eyes and slapped a black fly. She longed for the four o'clock breeze from the bay that would blow the pesky bugs away.

She looked up and saw Aunt Kit approaching with a red thermos and a wicker basket. "It's past two o'clock, and you didn't come up to the house for lunch. So I brought you some lemonade and sandwiches."

Boone scrambled up and pulled on his shirt. "Thanks. I'm parched. Starving, too." He took the picnic things from Kit and set them on the grass.

"There's two chicken salad and two ham," Kit said. "And a bunch of grapes. I put some cups and napkins in there, as well."

She took a long look at the wall. "You've made a heroic start. Don't overdo it, though. Miranda, you're not used to such heavy work."

Miranda stuck her thumb on her chest and wiggled her fingers. "I'm fine," she signed, twisting the cap off the thermos and pouring herself a big cup of lemonade.

Kit laughed. "That's what you say now, but wait till tomorrow morning when you're so stiff you can't get out of bed. Anyway, Boone's been at it since early this morning."

"I'm okay."

"Why don't you two call it a day after lunch? I insist. You'll find some money in the bottom of the picnic basket. Ride down to the village and get Mr. Leach to dish you up some ice cream. My treat."

Boone's face lit up. "Well, if you're sure . . ."

"I'm sure. Now I've got to get back to the studio." And she left Boone and Miranda alone together again.

Miranda rummaged through the picnic basket and dug out a chicken salad sandwich. She just wanted to eat her lunch and get away. As good as an ice cream cone sounded right now, she didn't think it was worth spending any more time with Boone than she absolutely had to.

Miranda chewed her sandwich.

Boone's face suddenly loomed in front of her own. "Are you going to hog it all, or can I have some?" he asked, grabbing the thermos and basket from Miranda.

Holding a half-eaten triangle of bread and chicken in one hand, Miranda started gesturing rapidly. She hadn't gotten everything Boone said, but the way he snatched the picnic things away from her made her angry.

Boone stared back at her. "Now what's the problem?" he snapped.

Miranda whipped out her pad and pencil. "It's your problem. You're rude."

"*I'm* rude?" Boone shouted. "You're so busy stuffing your face that you don't even think about sharing lunch."

Miranda's hands fell to her lap. It was true—she had taken a sandwich and poured herself a cup of lemonade without offering Boone anything.

But before she had a chance to say she was sorry, Boone erupted.

"Do you like being miserable? You're not the only one with problems, you know." He slopped some lemonade in a cup and gulped it down. "My mom's always so busy feeling sorry for herself that . . . well, never mind! I'm just sick of people feeling sorry for themselves, that's all."

Boone grabbed two plastic-wrapped packets and moved to the end of the rock wall to eat.

Miranda was stunned. Boone had talked so fast that she couldn't catch everything he said, but his anger came through loud and clear.

Maybe she *was* feeling sorry for herself.

They wolfed down their lunch, sitting apart with their backs to each other. They finished quickly, egged on by the black flies. Boone avoided looking at Miranda as they packed up their trash. He hurried back to the house ahead of her.

Miranda lagged behind. She supposed she ought to apologize. But when she reached the house, Boone and his bicycle were already gone. That meant she was going to have to ride down to the village to get that ice cream cone after all.

VII

By the time she flicked down the kickstand of her bike in front of Mr. Leach's store, Miranda was panting. Her leg muscles were cramping from having pumped her aunt's massive old bicycle. Besides, she didn't get much practice at home. "It's too dangerous," her mother said whenever Miranda begged to ride her bicycle. "You could turn in front of a car and not even hear it." After a while Miranda just left her bike in the garage.

Boone's bike was parked in the rack outside the store. Miranda shoved the screen door open and entered the dim coolness inside. Boone was nowhere to be seen.

Mr. Leach's store was nothing like the supermarket back in Virginia. Oak shelves rose to the ceiling, packed with all kinds of things for sale: hammers and fish hooks and bone china teacups, postcards and T-shirts and red plastic lobsters for the tourists, insect repellent and cans of shaving cream, comic books, even videotapes for rent. In a separate room to one side Mr. Leach stocked food: meat, eggs, butter, cartons of milk and juice, heads of lettuce, boxes of cereal, cans of soup. His store was a grocery, hardware store, and pharmacy all rolled into one.

Miranda's favorite part was the soda fountain. The granite-topped counter was right up front, near the door. Seven chrome stools with green vinyl seats swiveled around in circles. The menu board on the wall listed sandwiches, root beer floats, chocolate malteds, and Coke with cherry, vanilla, or lemon syrup squirted in it.

The ice cream cones were the best. There were only eight flavors to choose from, but the scoops were generous and the chunks of chocolate in the mint chip were huge.

Miranda hesitated. Neither Boone nor Mr. Leach was anywhere around. A blond, teenaged girl Miranda had never seen before stood behind the counter, busily mixing a milkshake. A boy about Miranda's age, dressed in khaki shorts and a yellow polo shirt, twirled back and forth on one stool. She recognized him as one of the rich summer people who lived in the big estates along the shore. Chad Thatcher—that was his name. He'd had it in for Miranda ever since the two of them collided in the Fourth of July boat race two summers ago.

Miranda let down her ponytail and began twirling it nervously into a long rope. She glanced around the store. She hoped Mr. Leach turned up before the girl finished making Chad's milkshake. Mr. Leach never had to ask what Miranda wanted. He just dug into the tub of mint chip ice cream when he saw her. Or if he wasn't around, then

Timothy was there to place her order.

But not this summer.

Miranda pushed that thought out of her head and watched as the girl poured Chad's shake out of the big silver mixing cup into a frosty glass. She rinsed out the cup, wiped her hands on a dish towel she wore tucked into the waist of her cutoffs like an apron, then turned to Miranda.

Miranda panicked. Oh, no. She craned her neck around. Where was Mr. Leach? Where was Boone?

If she spoke, the girl would never understand her. Because Miranda couldn't hear the sounds she was trying to make, she couldn't tell if they came out right. No one but her parents and teachers could ever figure out what she was saying.

She didn't want to write down what she wanted, either. That bothered her almost as much as the blank looks that people gave her when she tried to talk. She could feel their eyes on her, staring, or worse, pitying her.

Miranda could see the girl's mouth moving. She was asking Miranda what she wanted.

It wasn't worth it. She didn't want an ice cream cone after all. She shrugged and began to turn away when Chad tapped her on the shoulder.

She looked at his face.

"What's the matter?" he asked.

Miranda froze.

"Come on," he said. "Jenny here is waiting for your order." The girl behind the counter shifted her gaze back and forth between Chad and Miranda.

"Can I help you?" she asked.

Miranda shook her head and backed away.

Chad grabbed her arm. "I know you want something," he insisted, fishing a couple of crumpled dollar bills out of his shorts pocket. "It's on me. All you have to do is tell us what flavor you want."

Miranda felt her face grow hot. She wanted to get out of the store, but her legs wouldn't obey her brain. Her feet felt as if they were nailed to the floor.

"Maybe you ought to lighten up," Jenny said. "Maybe she doesn't want anything."

"Sure she does," Chad said. "She's just shy because she can't talk very well."

Miranda glared at him. She turned to the girl behind the counter. "Mint chip, please," she said. Her tongue felt thick and clumsy.

As soon as she opened her mouth, Miranda regretted it. She could tell from the look on Chad's face that it had sounded like gibberish.

Jenny frowned and shook her head. "I'm sorry, could you repeat that?"

"You just come back from the dentist over in Rockland or something?" Chad asked. "It sounds like the Novocaine hasn't worn off yet."

"Stop it!" Miranda shouted, chopping her right hand down on her left palm.

"Dob id!" Chad mocked her, then took a sip of his shake.

Miranda saw Chad's head swing around. She

turned too and saw Mr. Leach walk in from the side room where the groceries were sold. He joined Jenny behind the counter. Boone followed, carrying a brown paper bag. A loaf of bread and a roll of paper towels stuck out the top.

"What are you two making such an awful towse about?" Mr. Leach demanded.

Chad darted his eyes sideways at Miranda, then snuck a glance at Jenny. "Nothing, Mr. Leach. Sir." He smiled.

Mr. Leach lifted one bushy eyebrow. Without another word he plucked two paper-wrapped sugar cones from an upside-down stack and plunged a scoop into the tub of mint chip.

Miranda had lost her taste for ice cream. Her stomach felt as if it were filled with cement, but she gave a small nod and accepted the cone Mr. Leach gave her anyway.

While he dipped Boone's double maple walnut, Mr. Leach looked over at Chad and fixed him with a glinty stare. "You finished that frappe yet?"

Chad sucked up the last of his milkshake. "Yeah, I guess."

"'Bout time you headed home, ayuh? You sly on out now."

"If you say so." Chad slid off his stool, sauntered to the screen door, then yanked it open.

Miranda's ice cream started tasting better as soon as the door slammed behind Chad.

Mr. Leach rapped on the counter to get Miranda's attention. "Before you and the Thatcher boy got into a ruckus, I was telling Boone here about the Cheshire moon."

Miranda stiffened.

"You didn't finish," Boone said.

"It's an old island legend. The story's been around since my grandfather was a boy, maybe longer," Mr. Leach began as he wrung out a wet rag and started wiping down the granite. "Dreams have a way of coming real on Summerhaven. Especially when there's a Cheshire moon."

"That's a good one, Mr. Leach," Boone said, straining to smile. "I'll bet the tourists eat it up."

Miranda fumbled around in her pocket for her pad and pencil. "I don't think dreams come true anywhere," she wrote.

"Didn't say they come true," Mr. Leach replied. "Said they come *real*."

VIII

The tide surged across the narrow finger of land that jutted out into the bay. Everything but a cliff at the far end sank beneath the waves, turning the cliff into an island. Back on the main beach, Miranda was cut off by the rising water. Not now, she pleaded to the dream. She had almost made it.

On the wave-lashed island, grim spruce trees stood watch. Arched high above them, the river of stars that was the Milky Way glimmered in the inky blackness.

Time passed. Seconds, minutes, hours—Miranda could not tell. The muscles of her legs and shoulders strained tight as she waited for . . . what?

At last there was a great burst of light in the sky, like fireworks. Suddenly the sky was falling all around her, shooting stars blazing down like a rain of fire over the rocks and the waves. Miranda crouched down and covered her head with her hands.

Finally she peeked through her fingers, then looked up again. A bright figure, glowing with an unearthly light, walked out on the island.

It was a boy.

Miranda's heart skipped a beat.

"Turn around, turn around," she signed, circling her index fingers around each other. She needed to see his face.

The boy took a single step toward the trees.

"Wait!" she signed across the channel, holding her upturned palms in front of her and wiggling her fingers.

She stretched her arms out as the icy water swirled over her bare ankles and tugged at the hem of her nightgown. Yearning swelled inside her.

The boy kept walking away.

Miranda shook her head, whipping her hair behind her.

"Come back," she signed, sweeping her arms through the air and folding them into her chest. "Come back."

The boy disappeared into the woods, and the light died.

Miranda woke in pitch darkness. The memory of the dream weighed on her chest like a stone.

Boone pounded the pillow in frustration. That stupid dream again! The moon, and the race through the woods behind the blinking green-lit trail of fireflies.

He was sick of chasing Miranda each night in his dreams, sick of chasing her and never catching up.

Once again when he fell asleep, the light had streaked down behind his eyelids and plunged into the churning waters of the bay. Over on a small island Boone saw what looked like a star walking on the earth.

It was a boy. Boone couldn't see his face.

Boone plunged into the bone-chilling water, fighting the tide, but the waves beat him back. He couldn't get to the island.

Miranda was already there, a beat-up old canoe beached on the pebbled shore behind her.

"Don't!" Boone tried to warn her, but the words died in his throat. He had no voice. *You don't belong with him*, he wanted to shout. *You can't ever come back.*

But of course she couldn't have heard him anyway.

Miranda abandoned the canoe and began to walk toward the boy. She turned back for one moment, looking directly into Boone's eyes. She smiled.

Then he lost sight of her in the bright glow around the boy.

Boone glanced down into the waves at his feet. A half-submerged tree lay on the shore bottom, clawing up at him through the water like the skeleton of a dead man.

Boone shook himself completely awake. He bounded over to his desk, switched on the lamp, and grabbed a pencil out of an old orange juice can.

What was it about the boy on the island that seemed familiar?

Boone's hand flew over the paper.

• • •

Miranda rubbed her eyes and scratched a small lump behind her ear. The insect bites she had gotten yesterday while working on the rock wall were starting to itch. She scooted out of bed and shuffled toward the wall, where her clothes were hanging from a row of metal hooks. A sharp pain shot through her foot.

"Ow!" she burst out, aloud.

She had stepped on something hard.

Miranda squatted down to check what it was. A small black stone was wedged in a crack between the planks. She pried it loose to get a closer look.

With one finger Miranda rubbed the smooth, shiny crust that covered the stone. It looked almost as if the rock had melted.

"That's what shooting stars are," Timothy had told her. "Huge cinders of rock burning up as they plunge through the atmosphere."

It was a meteorite. Just like in her dream.

That couldn't be, Miranda scolded herself. Dreams happened in your mind. They weren't real. It was just a rock, an ordinary stone that must have been here all along. She just now found it, that's all.

It was just a coincidence—then suddenly she remembered the hem of her nightgown getting wet while she slept, and the the rockweed on the stairs, and the puddle by the front door.

Four coincidences?

Miranda shook her head. She wasn't ready to believe that her dreams were coming real, as Mr. Leach said.

She turned the dark stone over in her hand. So how had this ended up in her room?

Maybe she was sleepwalking. Maybe the tideswept island was real, and she had picked up the stone there. She could ask Aunt Kit.

But what if there was no island? Kit had already shown too much interest in Miranda's dreams. The last thing Miranda wanted was another adult—like her parents and teachers and weird old Dr. Stein—thinking there was something wrong with her.

She had to find out on her own. Perhaps somewhere on Summerhaven there was a rocky point that was cut off at high tide and turned into a temporary island.

Miranda tossed on a sleeveless blouse and a pair of striped shorts. She pocketed the meteorite. At least now there was something she could do about the dreams she'd been having. She could search for a place where meteorites had landed.

Her shoulders sagged when she realized how big a job this would be. Summerhaven was small—only four miles long and a mile across—but the shoreline was dotted with scores of headlands and coves. It would take her days to walk the island's jagged coast.

But there was no other way. There were no hills on the island, no central high point where she could get a bird's-eye view of the coastline.

And parts of the shore were private property, owned by people who didn't take kindly to trespassers.

Miranda chewed her lower lip. She slid her hand into her pocket and turned the stone over and over. Finally she began to smile.

Nobody owns the water, she thought. She knew what she would do.

IX

Frenchman's Cove lay flat and still, a blue mirror in which the trees and sky were doubled. Yellow pollen floated on top of the water like fairy dust. The air was cool.

A perfect day for canoeing, Miranda thought as she untied the slender red boat. Her plan was going to work.

She stowed a small cooler and a canteen in the canoe. She had packed an apple, a couple of cheese sandwiches, and a dill pickle for her lunch.

She pushed off the muddy floor of the cove and hopped into the boat. Kneeling on a piece of water-logged carpet, she leaned back against a cane seat in the stern. She picked up the paddle, dipped it in the water and pulled, propelling the canoe smoothly across the glasslike surface of the inlet.

She felt herself relax as she moved away from shore. It was peaceful out here alone.

She looked down. The water was so clear that Miranda could see several feet to the bottom. Small forests of hazel-green rockweed swayed beneath her. Tiny silver fish darted among the fronds.

Miranda steered the canoe toward the mouth of the cove. She had never done this by herself. She and Timothy had rarely strayed out into the bay, content to putter around the tamer waters inside the cove. But if there really was an island like the one in her dreams, this was the best way she could think of to search for it.

She realized her mistake as soon as the canoe entered the unprotected expanse of Penobscot Bay. A stiff breeze blew up. Waves churned the water, tossing out dirty gray flecks of foam. Miranda shuddered.

The canoe rocked wildly from side to side, threatening to swamp. Then it was caught in an unseen current and tugged relentlessly out into the bay.

Just like what had happened to Timothy.

Miranda looked down in the murky water. She should have worn a life jacket. But in the cold, heart-stopping waters of the bay, even a life jacket wouldn't save you for long.

Miranda dug her paddle into the water and struggled against the wind and the current. Waves sloshed over the sides and began to fill the boat.

The muscles in her arms and shoulders burned, but she dared not rest. If she stopped paddling for even a second, the canoe would be pulled farther out from shore.

Miranda paddled harder, attacking the water with each stroke. Her arms shook. Sweat poured down her face. She tucked her head down and saw nothing but the waves chopping and foaming around her.

Miranda raised her head for an instant. Was it wishful thinking, or did the mouth of the cove look closer? When she looked far back at the bluff, Aunt Kit's house did seem larger.

The sea sucked and dragged at the canoe. Miranda threw her whole body into the fight to break free, jabbing the paddle so deep in the water that it hauled her out of her seat. Finally, after what felt like hours, she broke free from the current and nosed the bow of the canoe back into the cove.

Almost at once the wind died down and the waves flattened out. Miranda paddled a short way. As the canoe drifted safely into calmer waters, she fell back against the stern, panting with exhaustion and relief.

It might take a lot longer, but she had better look for the dream island on foot after all.

Miranda sat up and began to paddle slowly back toward shore, resting every few strokes to give her aching arms a break. She was about a hundred yards out when she spotted Boone walking down the stairs from the top of the bluff.

Oh, no. He had seen her out here. He was sure to tell Aunt Kit.

Boone waded into shallow water as Miranda neared the shore. He signaled her to throw out the line in the bow of the boat.

Miranda took a few more strokes, then put down her paddle and did as Boone asked. He pulled the canoe up onto the beach and tied it to the nearest tree.

Miranda grabbed her lunch things and splashed into the water. She waited for Boone's lecture as she plopped down on a large flat rock.

Boone finished tipping the canoe to drain it and sat down beside her. He watched her for a long time, studying her pale, sweat-stained face.

"I go lobstering with old man Frechette sometimes," he said at last. "He hurt his back last winter, and he pays me a little to help him bring up his traps." Boone paused. "It kicks up rough before you know it out there."

Miranda's eyes widened. Boone could have said a lot more about how stupid she had been to take the canoe out of the cove in the first place, especially without a life jacket.

Miranda lay back and closed her eyes. She let the heat from the sun bathe her tired muscles. After a while a rumbling in her stomach forced her to sit up. She was hungry.

She took the two cheese sandwiches out of the cooler and offered one to Boone.

He touched his fingers to his lips, then pointed to Miranda.

Miranda stared at him, her mouth hanging open. Boone was full of surprises today. He had just signed "thank you" to her.

Boone took a bite of his sandwich and chewed it with a grin on his face.

Miranda dug down into her back pocket and fished out the pencil and a damp pad of paper. "Where did you learn that?"

Boone glanced down at the pad. "I checked out a book from the library."

Miranda raised her eyebrows. Boone *was* different. None of the kids at school ever showed enough interest to study a book on sign language.

"I only learned 'yes,' 'no,' 'please,' and 'thank you.' So far."

Miranda allowed herself a small smile.

"I thought you were hungry," Boone said. "Better eat your sandwich before I steal it."

They ate their lunch, taking turns swigging water from the canteen. Boone took out a pocketknife and cut the apple and the dill pickle in halves, and they shared those too.

He turned so that Miranda could see his face better. "Can I ask you a question without making you mad?"

Miranda nodded.

"How come you don't talk?"

Miranda frowned. "You heard me," she wrote. "You understood?"

"I was in the grocery side of the store, buying some things we needed at home. I really couldn't hear very well," Boone said. He glanced away.

Miranda poked his shoulder to make him turn back, then looked him steadily in the eye.

"Okay. I had a hard time making you out."

"Parents want me to talk, but I sound like a freak. Signing is . . ." Miranda paused and tapped her pencil against the pad, searching for the right word. ". . . natural."

"What do you mean, 'natural'?"

"How I think," she wrote. "In pictures, not words. But parents don't want me to sign."

Boone wrinkled his forehead. "I don't get it. Why don't they like sign language?"

"They're ashamed." Miranda pressed the pencil down hard into the paper. "I talk, they pretend I'm not deaf." The tip snapped off.

Boone took the pencil and began sharpening it with his pocketknife. "Maybe," he said. "Or maybe they just worry about you. About how you'll get along in the world."

Miranda looked out over the cove. Light danced off the rippling water and played across her face. She had never thought of it that way. Her parents, not ashamed of her being deaf, but worried.

Miranda took the pencil back from Boone. "Makes no difference. Talking—big waste. Quit last year."

Boone picked up a pebble and skipped it across the water.

"Why?" he asked, facing Miranda. "What happened last year?"

Miranda shrugged. "Just decided, after Timothy—" She broke off.

Boone looked Miranda directly in the eyes. "I met him, you know."

Miranda tilted her head to one side.

"Just once. Mom moved us over from Portsmouth at the start of September, and Timothy's parents weren't due here until Labor Day. Where were you?"

Miranda grimaced. "School starts early back home in Virginia," she wrote.

"He seemed like a nice guy," Boone went on. "I helped look for him; everybody did. I'm sorry about what happened."

Miranda caught her bottom lip between her teeth and bit down. What good did being sorry do? Timothy was still dead. She swallowed until the painful lump in her throat was gone.

"He was best friend," she wrote. "Signed like deaf."

"Maybe you could teach me to sign someday."

Miranda stared out at the water.

Boone waited, then tapped Miranda on the shoulder.

She turned to look at him.

"Do you know that rock pool down-island?" Boone asked.

Miranda nodded. She and Timothy used to swim there.

Standing two fingers on the back of one hand, Boone pantomimed a person diving into the water.

Miranda rolled her eyes. "No, no," she signed, snapping her fingers at him with a laugh. Then she circled her hands in front of her as if she were doing the breast stroke.

"Give me a break, I don't have a book here to look these things up," Boone said. "The point is, do you want to go swimming?" And he did the breast stroke through the air too.

Maybe a swim was a good idea. She was hot and filthy and covered with bug bites. A dip would cool her off.

Miranda jammed her hand in her front pocket and rubbed the meteorite she'd put there this morning. That seemed like days ago now.

But she hadn't forgotten the dream. Miranda scribbled a note and handed it to Boone. "Any little islands off Summerhaven?"

Boone stared at the note for a long time before raising his head to speak. "Why do you ask that?"

Boone sure had a funny look on his face, Miranda thought. She tore off the top page of her notepad and began folding the paper into ever-smaller triangles. Maybe she had made a mistake asking him about the island.

She turned both palms up in the air and shrugged. "Just wondering," she wrote. "Go get suits."

Miranda hurried up the steps to the top of the bluff.

X

From her lookout high atop a granite boulder, Miranda shaded her eyes and scanned the landscape around her. Boone floated on his back in a tidal pool nearby. Heaps of seaweed, long brown strands drying in the sun, smothered the rocks below. It looked as if some giant shaggy beast lay napping there with its paws in the sea.

Nothing looked familiar. There was no cliff at the end of a finger of land, no place that the rising tide could cut off and turn into an island.

Miranda dropped her hands and sighed. She shouldn't have gotten her hopes up. Summerhaven had many miles of coastline to explore. She would have to keep searching.

Miranda took one last look. There was no point in staying any longer. She wrapped her towel around her like a blanket and clambered down the rocks.

Boone scrambled after her. They trudged back to their bicycles, pulled their clothes on over their damp swimsuits, and headed home.

"Can we stop by my house for a minute?" Boone asked.

Miranda made a face, not having understood. She

couldn't ride a bike and read lips at the same time.

Boone signaled for her to turn. She coasted a moment, hesitating, then followed him onto a dirt path that led back through a field of weeds to an old house. They dropped their bikes in the long grass.

Boone's house had once been white, Miranda could tell from the scabs of paint that still clung to the wood. But now it was weathered gray from years of wind and rain and salt air. Broken shutters dangled from the windows.

Boone held open the back door for Miranda. The screen was torn. "Place needs some work," he said. "But since Grampa fell and broke his hip, I can't keep up around here."

Miranda took her pad out of her pocket. "Dad help?"

Boone's face darkened. "Pop walked out on us last year. That's when my mom brought us back here from New Hampshire to live with her folks."

So that was what Boone had meant when he yelled at her yesterday in Aunt Kit's garden that other people had problems too. Miranda rubbed her fist on her chest in a circle. "Sorry," she wrote.

"It's no big deal. We're better off without him."

They walked into the kitchen. Miranda wrinkled her nose. It smelled of sour milk. A pile of dirty plates and cups tottered in the sink.

"Jeez, Jeremy, you were supposed to wash the lunch dishes," Boone shouted into the next room, where four kids were clustered in front of a television set.

Miranda saw the muscles along Boone's jaw working under the skin.

She pointed to herself, then rubbed her hands together as if she were washing something. She tilted her head toward the sink.

Boone waved away her offer of help. "No, thanks. It'll get done." He moved over to a back stairway that led out of the kitchen. "Come on. I've got something to show you."

Miranda hung back a moment, trailing behind as Boone bolted up the stairs to the second floor, and then up a rickety set of steps to the attic. The ceiling sloped down low on two sides, forcing Boone and Miranda to duck. Foil-covered blankets of pink insulation were stapled to the walls.

Miranda raised her fists to her shoulders and shook them slightly. She wrote, "Cold in winter?"

Boone shook his head. "It's not bad. The heat from that chimney keeps it fairly warm." He rummaged through a makeshift desk fashioned out of two dented filing cabinets with a board lying across them.

Miranda glanced around the room. Prints of famous paintings and posters from art museums were tacked to the rafters in the ceiling. The one right over Boone's bed was by van Gogh.

Miranda gazed at the swirls of blue and yellow that van Gogh had used to paint the night sky. Timothy would have liked that, she thought.

Abruptly, she turned away from the poster and walked over to the window. Outside, birch leaves fluttered and danced in the breeze, breaking the long shafts of sunlight into gold-tinged shadows that trembled across Miranda's face.

Boone picked up his sketch pad and, studying her, began to draw. After a while he put down his pencil and moved beside her. "What are you looking at?" he asked.

Miranda made a V sign with her fingers, touched her eyes, and gestured toward the window.

"Watch," she said hoarsely.

Boone's mouth sagged open. "What did you say?"

Miranda felt the blood rush to her face. She hadn't meant to speak. The word just slipped out before she'd thought about it.

Like it did sometimes with Timothy.

It was a mistake. Of course Boone couldn't understand her. She brushed her fingers against his temple and pointed outside.

Boone nodded.

Miranda grabbed her pad. "Leaves, light—see how they move?"

Boone looked out the window.

"Like a song," Miranda wrote. She waved her arms gracefully back and forth in time with the wind and the tree, tracing figure-eights with her hands. "Eye music."

Boone walked back to his desk and picked up a thick sheaf of paper, nodding once to himself as if he had made up his mind. He handed the stack of papers to Miranda. "I've got something to show you, too."

She leafed through the drawings slowly. They were sketches Boone had penciled of Summerhaven. There were pictures of lobster boats bobbing in the harbor near the ferry wharf, and of an abandoned lighthouse crumbling into the sea.

There were portraits too. Boone had drawn several versions of the same picture: a tall, black-haired man, shoulders hunched, standing in a doorway. In each of the pictures the man's face was blurred—erased and redone, over and over.

Boone watched Miranda's reaction, then bent his head down so his face was in her line of view. "That's my father," he said.

Miranda scribbled on her pad. "Is he coming in or going out?" she asked.

"I don't know," Boone said, jamming his hands in his pockets. "I can't get it right. No matter how many times I try, his face . . . something about his eyes . . . it's all wrong."

Miranda didn't know what to say. Uncomfortable, she flipped over the last portrait of Boone's father. Staring up at her from the page beneath was her own face.

Miranda's hands shook. She clutched the picture tightly in her fingers and let the rest of the stack drop to the floor.

"Something wrong?" Boone asked.

Miranda stared at her image on the paper. It was as if she were looking in a mirror and seeing herself for the first time.

She scowled. What was she doing here with Boone? She'd only met him a couple of days ago—too soon to be acting like friends.

Not the way she and Timothy had been.

Miranda ripped the drawing in half, balling up the pieces and tossing them on the floor.

"What do you think you're doing?" Boone howled. He grabbed her wrists and shook her. "I drew that. You had no right to tear it up."

Miranda yanked her hands free and began signing, punching her arms wildly through the air at Boone. She snatched her pad and scrawled, "Lousy picture. Doesn't look like me anyway."

She ran out of the room and hurtled downstairs.

Miranda hunched over the handlebars, rising off the seat of the bike and pressing her full weight down on the pedals. She blew out hard each time she pumped her legs. She couldn't get away from Boone's house fast enough.

The last traces of the sunset festered in the sky, red and angry as a hornet's sting. A bluish-purple curtain of dusk began to fall. The moon stared down overhead, four days fatter than it had been Miranda's first night on Summerhaven. Its smile was almost gone. In another day or two it would be a half moon.

Her eyes on the Cheshire moon, Miranda skidded on a patch of loose gravel. The handlebars jerked out of her grip and the bike lurched sideways. She tumbled forward, sprawling on the ground.

73

Miranda picked herself up and brushed off her clothes. Her knee burned. She reached down and felt wet skin through a tear in her jeans. Great—she was bleeding and had just ruined her favorite pair of jeans.

She squinted at the bike through the dusk and ran her hands along the frame. A jet of air from the front tire rushed against her fingers. She had a flat.

Miranda hit herself in the forehead with the back of her fist, signing "Stupid!" She grunted and started pushing the bike down the path.

She trudged back to Aunt Kit's house as the last red and purple light drained from the sky, her thoughts swirling like tea leaves in a cup.

Miranda limped down the drive and came in sight of the house. Buttery light streamed through the kitchen window and cast a bright elongated square in the back yard. She could see her Aunt Kit bent over the sink, getting dinner ready.

Her aunt raised her head and waved, holding a half-scrubbed carrot aloft.

Miranda propped the bicycle against the outside wall of the studio and looked up at the second-floor window of the house. Timothy's room. The dark glass stared back at her blankly.

She tried to imagine Timothy's face in the window, but nothing came. She could not picture him. All she got was a fuzzy smear, like the sketch Boone had drawn of his father. Timothy was nothing but a blur.

Miranda's throat tightened. She was forgetting

him. He had been dead only nine months, and already she couldn't remember what he looked like.

It shouldn't be so easy to forget your best friend.

Miranda kicked the wall of the studio, shaking dirt and dead leaves down from the eaves, then went inside to dinner. She wasn't hungry. She just wanted to go to bed.

XI

The Cheshire moon grinned one last time and dipped below the horizon. In the big iron bed upstairs, Miranda's eyes jumped back and forth under her lids. Her hands fluttered through the air, making signs that no one was there to see. With a shudder, she kicked off the quilt.

The dream had come for her again.

A ghostly cloud of light shimmered on the lawn, luring her through the gloom until suddenly she was *there*—standing on the stony beach, staring across the channel at the island where she had seen stars rain down on the earth.

A battered green canoe waited for Miranda. She stepped in and picked up a paddle, gliding easily across the inlet to the island with just a few strokes.

Miranda looked back and saw Boone chasing after her. He stumbled, dragged down by the skeleton of a tree that lay half-drowned along the beach. One clawlike branch lashed against his face. A dark red stripe of blood welled up on his left cheek.

The canoe bumped against the bottom on the opposite shore. Miranda stepped out and picked her way carefully among the rocks on the beach to the edge of the dark spruce woods.

The boy was already waiting for her.

"Come closer, come closer," she signed. "Let me see your face."

The boy edged out from beneath the trees. It was Timothy.

Boone yanked the covers over his head and heaved himself onto one side, bedsprings squeaking loudly in the silence.

Forget about the stupid dream. He shouldn't let it bother him.

But it did.

Boone staggered over to the desk and fumbled in the dark for the string that switched on the light bulb overhead.

Ignoring a twinge of pain on the left side of his face, he tore a clean sheet of paper off a pad. He dumped out the orange juice can full of pencils and began to sketch furiously.

He filled several pages with rough images: a phantom canoe drifting away from shore; two shadowy figures walking on a wave-tossed island; a water-logged tree with branches like long, twisted fingers.

Boone stopped and stared at what he had drawn. He knew Miranda was one of the figures on the island, but who was the other? He cocked his head and turned the paper sideways, looking at the picture from a different angle.

More slowly now Boone moved his pencil,

sketching and shading. He snatched an eraser and rubbed out a few lines, cleaning off the page with a sweep of his hand. A tall, lean figure began to emerge.

But still it had no face.

Boone continued to draw, outlining eyes, nose, mouth. He dropped the pencil and frowned.

It was Miranda's cousin Timothy. The one who had been lost in the vast, cold waters of the bay. Whose battered, empty canoe Mr. Leach had found washed up at the far end of Summerhaven.

Why was he dreaming about someone he had met only once?

If only he could remember more.

Clamping a pencil in his mouth, Boone gathered the sketches he had just made and added them to the pile from the past few mornings. It was just a dream. Stop thinking about it. It didn't matter if Miranda canoed off to an imaginary island to meet the ghost of her cousin.

He glanced at the edge of his desk. The crumpled halves of the portrait that Miranda had destroyed lay there. Boone smoothed them out and fitted the pieces together as best he could. Her face was skewed: nose crooked, mouth twisted out of line, one eye slightly lower than the other. The picture was past fixing, even if he tried to tape it back together. He would have to start from scratch.

Boone sighed. He stashed his pencils back in the orange juice can and dug some clothes out of a drawer. He plodded downstairs to the bathroom to brush his teeth.

When he caught a glimpse of his face in the mirror, he dropped his toothbrush in the sink.

There was a fresh scratch on his left cheek.

XII

Miranda anchored the pump between her feet and plunged the handle down, forcing a blast of air into the patched front tire of her bicycle. Her face drooped.

Just when she wanted to believe Mr. Leach's story about dreams coming real, the proof had evaporated. She had awakened this morning and found no trace of it.

No wet nightgown, no clumps of rockweed, no telltale puddles of seawater. Nothing.

Miranda felt a tap on her shoulder and turned to see Aunt Kit wave good morning as she passed into the studio. A streak of crimson paint stained the bib of her white overalls.

Miranda stopped pumping.

Red paint. Red in the dream. The dark red stripe of blood on Boone's left cheek.

Miranda capped off the tire and raced inside the studio. She thrust a piece of paper at Aunt Kit. "Where's Boone?"

Four seconds later Miranda jumped on her bike and shot down the drive to the harbor. If the dream was coming real, maybe Boone would have the proof she hoped for.

• • •

Miranda stood on the wharf and jammed her hands into her pockets, rubbing the meteorite like a worry stone. Down on the floating dock, Boone unloaded the last of the lobster traps from Mr. Frechette's boat and strode up a gangplank to the main pier.

He pulled off his Red Sox cap to wipe the sweat from his forehead, and turned. Miranda saw his cheek.

She blinked hard, twice, and gripped the meteorite so tightly that it bit into her palm.

A jagged scratch, just beginning to scab over, ran down the left side of Boone's face.

"It is real," she signed, sinking down on top of a massive wooden post that supported the wharf. "You were there, too."

Boone shook his head. "I don't understand."

Miranda tugged him down on the piling beside her and took out her pad and paper. "You dreamt island."

Boone sucked in his breath sharply. His face blanched, making the brownish-red of the cut stand out in stark relief against his skin.

Miranda jabbed him in the chest. She wrote, "Fireflies in woods, beach, Timothy's canoe—"

Boone grabbed the pencil out of her hand. "How can we be having the same dream?"

She snatched the pencil back. "Don't know. Cheshire moon?" She made a large C with her thumb and forefinger, touched it to her temple, and lifted it above her head. Then she traced a smile across her lips with the fingers of both hands.

"I've seen it," Boone said. "And I know what Mr. Leach said about dreams coming to life, but that's just an act to impress the summer people."

He folded his arms across his chest. "People used to think that the moon could drive you crazy. That's where the word 'lunatic' comes from."

He tilted his head toward Miranda and cocked one eyebrow.

"Both crazy," she scrawled across her pad, glowering at him defiantly. "If dreams not real, then how this?"

Miranda brushed her finger across the scratch on his cheek.

"I *saw* you trip on tree," she wrote. "In dream. Didn't you?"

Boone swallowed and caught his lower lip between his teeth.

"Woke up yesterday, found this." Miranda brandished the meteorite like a trophy under Boone's nose. "Shooting star—you know where."

Boone took the shiny black stone from Miranda and examined it, turning it over in his hands.

"Found rockweed, seawater in house too."

"Summerhaven is an island," Boone said. "There is seaweed and salt water all over the place. You could have been sleepwalking and bringing that stuff back with you."

"Both sleepwalk?" Miranda cast him a sour look. "Same dream every night?"

Boone shifted uncomfortably on the piling, as if the wooden post were bristling with splinters.

"I did find some crushed shells in the bottom of my bed one morning," he admitted. "I didn't think much about it then, but now . . ." He touched his cheek. "It was like I'd been out walking barefoot on a beach. And I had—in my dream."

Miranda didn't catch everything Boone said. "You believe me?" she wrote.

As Boone answered, he began pacing the wharf. Miranda followed and circled in front of him, bringing him to an abrupt halt. Frowning and shaking her head, she pointed to her eyes.

"Sorry." Boone flashed a brief smile of apology. "I said there's got to be some logical explanation. This is just too weird. Dreams don't actually happen. They're just your brain making up stories."

"Two brains, same story?" Miranda wrote.

"Okay, so that still doesn't make sense." Boone's face fell. "Maybe one of the doctors my mom works with could figure it out."

"No!" Miranda scrawled. She could picture the look on Dr. Frankenstein's face if she'd come up with a story like this during one of their Thursday afternoon counseling sessions. He would purse his lips and write "hallucination" down in his notes, with a gleam in his eye.

"What about your aunt? We could talk to her."

Miranda shook her head vehemently. Not Aunt Kit—she couldn't tell her. It was bad enough having her parents and teachers mad at her all the time. She didn't want that to happen with Aunt Kit, too.

"Nobody would believe us," she wrote.

"I'm not sure I believe us," Boone said.

Miranda gritted her teeth. Something wondrous was going on in their dreams, but all Boone wanted to do was pick them apart and make them ordinary.

She needed someone who knew all about the old Summerhaven legends. Someone who could tell her more about the Cheshire moon and dreams and mysteriously appearing islands.

Mr. Leach.

Miranda wrote down his name and handed it to Boone.

Boone rolled his eyes. "Mr. Leach is the one who put these ideas into your head in the first place. We're not going to get a logical explanation from him."

Miranda jumped to her feet. "Forget logic!" she wrote. "Leach knows—he might help."

"Help what?" Boone asked, narrowing his eyes.

Miranda hesitated. "Find the island."

"Was that what you were doing out in the canoe yesterday?"

Miranda nodded. "After Leach, borrow Frechette's boat?"

Boone's face darkened. "I don't think that's such a good idea."

"Why not?" Surely Boone longed to get back to the dream as much as she did.

"Because it's . . . it's dangerous, that's all."

Miranda burst out laughing. "What danger?"

She waved one arm above her head and looked up with a rapt expression on her face. Now more than ever she wanted to find that island where stars rained down out of the sky. She needed to find it.

Maybe she would find Timothy there.

But she couldn't tell Boone that. He was still clinging to his doubts as stubbornly as a barnacle to a rock. He didn't want to believe that the dreams were coming real.

Miranda cradled the meteorite in her palm. "Something wonderful will happen there, I know it," she wrote.

Boone's eyes clouded over. He fingered the cut on his cheek and flinched.

"I don't think we're having the same dream after all," he said.

XIII

The screen door to Mr. Leach's store swung out on a sudden gust of wind when Miranda and Boone rode up, as if an invisible hand were opening it for them. The store was empty, shadows lurking in every corner.

"This is a waste of time," Boone said. "I've got work to do. Let's come back tomorrow."

Mr. Leach appeared from the back of the store, rifling through a stack of letters. "Here for some ice cream?" he asked.

Boone shook his head. "No, sir."

"What do you want then?"

Boone nudged Miranda with his elbow. "She wants to ask you a question."

"Ayuh?" Mr. Leach stepped behind the soda fountain and picked up a metal scoop. He began scraping down the sides of a half-empty ice cream tub.

Miranda dug into her pocket for her notepad and stub of pencil and slapped them down on the sandwich counter. The granite felt cold beneath her fingers.

Mr. Leach scowled. "Don't have all day."

Miranda swallowed hard and began to write.

"Remember Cheshire moon?" She slid the pad across the counter.

Mr. Leach arched one bushy eyebrow. "I'm not so old that I don't recollect what I say to folks."

Boone cleared his throat. "Of course not, sir."

Miranda looked up at Mr. Leach uncertainly. "Is there more to story?"

Mr. Leach stretched his lips into a scant smile, and his face broke into a thousand wrinkles. "Summerhaven's haunted, you know," he said.

Miranda glanced over at Boone.

"By dreams, not ghosts," Mr. Leach went on. "The Indians believed that the island was a place of powerful magic—especially when there was a Cheshire moon. They sent their sick here for visions they thought would cure them."

The muscles in Boone's jaw slackened. "So this *is* just an old island legend," he said.

Mr. Leach pinched his eyebrows together and gazed steadily down his nose at Boone. "Some folks on Summerhaven still get those dreams."

Boone took a step backward.

"There's an island," Miranda wrote rapidly, "offshore. How get there?"

"New Moon Island?" Mr. Leach said. "How'd you hear about that? You can't get there."

"Why not?" Boone asked.

"It's not on the charts anymore." Mr. Leach leaned across the granite counter and towered over them.

"The coast of Maine is slowly sinking," he said.

87

"Three feet every century. You can't get to New Moon Island because it sank beneath the waves over a hundred years ago."

Boone stalked out of the store and rode straight to Kit's garden, pedaling his bike as if he were being chased by a demon. Miranda was hard pressed to catch up.

He dropped a stone on the rock wall with a resounding *thunk*.

"Need to find island," Miranda wrote. "This didn't come from nowhere." She plucked the meteorite out of her pocket.

Boone brushed his hands on his jeans and turned to face her. "Look, Miranda," he began. "I think you want this dream to be real so bad that you'll believe anything."

"What do you mean?" she wrote.

Boone threw his hands up in the air. "You could have picked up that rock anywhere. As for Mr. Leach's story, well . . ."

Miranda scowled.

"You can ask your Aunt Kit about Mr. Leach. He likes to think of himself as the Edgar Allan Poe of Summerhaven. If he thought you really believed all this business about smiling moons and haunted islands, he'd probably tell you himself that he's just pulling your leg."

Miranda felt her cheeks burning. What did Boone know?

"Now, come on," Boone said. "Are you going to

help me with this wall or not?"

"Forget it!" Miranda signed, wiping her hand angrily across her forehead as if she were wiping all thought of Boone out of her mind.

Miranda spent the rest of the afternoon prowling aimlessly around the house. She didn't want Boone to be right, but maybe—just maybe—he was. Maybe she was letting wishful thinking get in the way of common sense.

Dead was dead. Timothy had gone out canoeing one day and never come back. Did she really think she would find him in a lightstorm on some mysterious island?

Miranda wandered into Timothy's room and drew a circle in the dust on his desk.

Dust we are, and unto dust we shall return. Isn't that what the rector had said at Timothy's memorial service?

Miranda looked at the row of tattered, well-thumbed books on the shelf above the desk. She began to straighten them, and her glance fell on *The Golden Guide to the Stars.*

She took down the book, flipping through the pages to a table listing the dates of meteor showers recurring every year.

One line in the table jumped out at her. "Pegasid meteor shower," it read. "June 24-26. Radiating from the Great Square of Pegasus."

Miranda closed her eyes and smiled. Everything fell into place.

This was what the dream had been trying to tell her all along. Tonight was the night.

Toweling his hair dry from the shower, Boone climbed the steps to his bedroom. He sank down at the window, exhausted after a long afternoon hauling rocks, and peered out at the night sky.

The quarter moon hung low in the west. It didn't look to Boone as if it were smiling. The bright curve had grown until it covered almost half the moon's surface.

A streak of light arced across the sky.

Boone stiffened. A shooting star.

As he watched, he saw a second light flash across the heavens, then a third.

The sky is falling, Boone thought. Tonight— there's a meteor shower tonight.

He grabbed his jeans and sneakers and fumbled through one of his desk drawers for a flashlight.

When Miranda saw the stars streaking across the sky, she would set off on her own to find an island that had slumbered on the bottom of the bay for over a century.

Because the boy on that ghostly island was her drowned cousin, Timothy.

If Boone didn't keep his eye on her, Miranda might end up drowning too.

XIV

The wind lashed the branches of the oak against the bedroom window, leaves fidgeting madly in the troubled air. Miranda jiggled one leg under the quilt. She rolled over on her side and punched her pillow for the umpteenth time that night. She was too keyed up to fall asleep.

The Cheshire moon peeked in through the window. Miranda crept across the bed and looked outside. Her mouth dropped open. A great cloud of light hovered over the lawn, winking at her with a thousand eyes.

Fireflies! Just like in her dream.

But this time she was wide awake.

Miranda's heart somersaulted in her chest. It was happening. The dream was coming real.

She bounded out of bed and raced down to the front lawn, dew-soaked grass chilling her bare feet. Fireflies weaved in and out of her hair and beat their wings against her face.

As she stood in the midst of the cloud, it changed shape, narrowing and stretching into a column of light to guide her through the woods.

She sprinted into the forest. Branches slapped her face and snatched at her ankles as she followed the living neon trail. Fallen needles pricked her feet.

Miranda stumbled over a pine root and fell. The ancient deep smell of the forest, a musty perfume of rotting leaves and dank earth, filled her nose.

Spitting dirt out of her mouth, Miranda wiped her face with a grimy hand and lurched to her feet. She started to run again. Her soles were blistered and bleeding by the time she broke past the trees and staggered out on the stones of the beach. Miranda bent over, bracing her arms against her thighs, and took a long shuddering breath.

The tide had already come in. The moon's reflection was scattered over the waves.

Miranda lifted her head. There across the channel was New Moon Island.

And then the light came, pounding down from the sky. Miranda curled up like a snail and shielded her head with her hands. All around her stars plunged into the bay sending up ribbons of steam.

When at last she lowered her hands and dared to look up, an empty green canoe floated in the shallows offshore.

It was waiting for her.

Boone switched off his flashlight and skulked down the drive to Miranda's house. An owl hooted a warning. Crickets chirred and frogs croaked in a duet that pulsed like the beating of some giant woodland heart: *creek-boom, creek-boom.*

Boone snuck around to the front of the house and froze. His eye was caught by a faint greenish glimmer flashing in the distance. A line of fireflies snaked through the trees—just like in the dream.

But these fireflies were real. He chased after them.

The night closed in around him as he ran, squeezing the breath out of his lungs and filling his ears with painful pressure. All he could think was *get there, get there, hurry.*

Boone crashed out of the woods.

Hundreds of stars pelted down from the sky. Boone fell to his knees. The sky was ablaze with light. Blinded, he covered his eyes and bowed his head. Colors still blossomed behind his eyelids, exploding like fireworks.

When at last he looked up, the night looked darker than ever.

And there across the channel loomed the island that should not exist—except in his dreams.

Boone's heart pounded. There wasn't time to run all the way back to the harbor and borrow Mr. Frechette's boat. The only way to get to New Moon Island was to swim.

Boone tugged off his shoes and socks and threw them aside. He waded out, gasping at the first shock of cold. But Boone had no choice. He sucked in his breath and splashed out into the channel, feeling the blood thicken in his veins as he ducked his head beneath the waves.

He set off with powerful, sure strokes, plowing through the water as fast as he could.

But all too soon the cold seeped into his body.

His arms and legs grew leaden and sluggish. A thunderous roar echoed in his ears. Each breath knifed through his lungs.

He toiled forward across the channel, but the waves piled higher and higher on top of him, and the cold stole deeper and deeper inside him.

Boone stopped fighting and treaded water. The gap between him and the island seemed wider than when he started.

He was cold, so cold.

Boone lifted one arm over his head and dropped it down in the water. He gave his legs a final kick.

He wasn't going to make it.

XV

The icy water raised goosebumps on her legs as Miranda stepped out of the canoe. She flexed her knees and bounced up and down, testing the ground to assure herself it was solid. She was finding it hard to believe that New Moon Island was real.

Miranda looked around uneasily, twisting her nightgown between her fingers. She was all alone here. Alone in the dark on an island that could, at any minute, sink back under the waves.

Boone was right. The moon must have made her crazy. She ought to take the canoe and head back to Summerhaven.

Light glowed from a stand of spruce up-island. Miranda swallowed hard. This could be what she had longed for since that terrible day when her father told her that Timothy was dead.

Miranda walked up the beach and into the woods, wandering blindly through the trees until she reached a clearing in the center of the island.

A blaze of light dazzled her as she walked out from the shelter of the spruces. She shaded her eyes and squinted into the blue-white glare. She could just make out a solitary figure waiting there.

The light, although it did not dim, grew less harsh.

"Is that better?"

Clapping her hands to her ears, Miranda jerked her head around. Had she heard that?

"No," the voice sounded. "We share each other's thoughts, heart to heart."

Miranda stared down at the grass at her feet. She was strangely reluctant to look at the shining figure.

"Look up." Featherlike, the words touched her.

Slowly, hesitantly, she lifted her eyes. Miranda forgot to breathe.

It was Timothy.

Timothy. Except for the incandescent white glow that seemed to emanate from every part of him, he looked exactly the same as he did last August when they said good-bye on the ferry.

"Are you a ghost?" Miranda pinched the thumb and finger of her right hand together and pulled them out of her cupped left hand. "Or an angel?" She brushed her fingertips off each shoulder.

Timothy laughed. Miranda could feel it, like a creek rippling over a bed of pebbles. The feeling was not unpleasant, but right now it was making her dizzy.

"I'm as real as your dreams," Timothy told her.

Miranda rubbed her temples. She had so many questions her head felt as though it would burst. But there was only one question that mattered.

"Did you come back to stay?"

Timothy didn't answer.

"Don't you want things the way they used to be?" she asked.

Timothy looked at her with the eyes she remembered so well, saying nothing.

"You were the only one I could ever talk to," she said at last, her hands dancing, slipping back into signs again.

"What about him?" Timothy asked, gazing over her shoulder.

Miranda spun around and saw nothing but the dark wall of spruce trees standing guard behind her. "Who?"

"Boone." The hairs on the back of her neck prickled. "He's washed up on the beach. He thought he needed to save you."

The bitter acid taste of guilt flooded Miranda's mouth. Don't let it be because of me that anything happens to Boone, she thought.

Miranda hurtled through the stand of spruce to the beach. There was a crumpled form by the water's edge. Boone.

She knelt over Boone's limp body, then rolled him over on his side and pounded his back. A stream of water trickled out of his mouth. She laid her cheek against his lips to feel for the outrush of air. Nothing.

"Breathe!" She yelled it out loud at the top of her voice. "Breathe, Boone!" She could feel the words scraping the back of her throat.

He gasped, then started to retch. Miranda

crouched beside him. His skin was clammy and gray.

The air around her brightened and she turned to see Timothy standing behind her on the beach.

"He's so cold. He needs dry clothes and a blanket. Can't you do anything?" Miranda begged.

Timothy shook his head.

"If we don't do something soon, he could die," Miranda said. She looked around frantically and spotted the canoe.

Timothy nodded. "It will carry you back to Summerhaven."

"Will you still be here when I get back?"

Timothy was silent, but Miranda already knew the answer.

Her throat constricted. No matter what she chose to do, she would lose something.

She could stay with Timothy. It felt so wonderful to be heard, heart to heart, without having to translate everything into the difficult language of sound.

But what would happen to Boone?

Miranda stared grimly into the darkness and noticed a thin line of light on the eastern horizon. Dawn was approaching.

Miranda clasped Boone's hand and hauled him to his feet. The coldness of his skin told her there wasn't much time. She draped his arm around her neck and, staggering under his weight, propped her shoulder beneath him like a crutch.

"I've got to get him home," she said.

Miranda dragged the ashen boy across the beach and lifted him into the bow of the boat.

The tide was going out, and the edges of the island—the pebbles on the beach, the spires of the spruce trees—seemed to fluctuate in and out of sight.

As if dawn were erasing the island. As if it were fading back into the dream from which it came.

Miranda gripped the side of the canoe.

"I carry a part of you with me wherever I go," Timothy said. "And you keep a part of me—the realest, truest part."

Miranda bit her lip, and her eyes blurred with tears. The air felt too thick to breathe.

Timothy swept two fingers from his eyes and touched Miranda lightly over the heart. "But whenever you want me, look in. That's where you'll find me."

Miranda clutched his fingers with both hands. Gently he pulled them free.

And then Timothy was gone.

Tears tracked silently down her face. Her head drooped, and she noticed that the stones under her feet had become transparent. New Moon Island was disappearing.

Boone tugged at the sleeve of her nightgown. Miranda squeezed his shoulder. How much longer would he make it if she didn't get him home? She shoved the canoe into the water, then jumped in herself.

She did not look back until the canoe had ferried them across the channel and was beached back on Summerhaven.

Hugging him to keep him warm, Miranda helped Boone up the shore as the canoe slid out and sank beneath the waves.

New Moon Island flickered in and out of view. For one moment Miranda could see the yellow ribbon of dawn through the vanishing trunks of the trees. Then the island was gone.

XVI

The acrid smell of oil smoke from the outboard motor stung Miranda's nose as the skiff chugged into Frenchman's Cove. The August sun blazed overhead, bleaching the sky a faded denim blue. Sweat trickled down her face, leaving salty tracks she could taste in the corners of her mouth.

Miranda swiveled around to face Boone, who sat in the stern steering the boat.

"Wait," she signed, holding both hands palm up in front of her and wiggling her fingers. "Can we stop here a minute?"

Boone throttled down the engine and switched it off. Instantly the beelike buzz Miranda had been feeling in her bones ended. The boat slowed to a stop and began to bob up and down on the waves.

Miranda tucked her hand into her left pocket and dug out two small pieces of beige plastic.

Boone leaned forward. "I didn't know you use hearing aids." His signing was slower than Miranda's, stiffer, but after a summer of practice he moved his hands with confidence. "I've never seen you wear them."

"I don't. Not anymore."

She stretched her hand out over the water and

tilted it. The hearing aids began to slide across her palm.

"No!" Boone shouted, lunging forward. He leaned over the side of the boat and cupped his hand a few inches beneath Miranda's. The ear molds slipped out of her hand and fell safely into his.

Boone lowered himself back in the boat and stared at Miranda. His face was pale. "These must cost a fortune," he signed.

She shrugged.

"You could get in a lot of trouble throwing these away."

"I am deaf." Miranda swept one finger from her ear to her closed lips. "Everybody thinks that means I'm broken," she signed. "They think those"—she pointed to the hearing aids in Boone's fist—"will fix me. But I'm not broken. I can hear with my eyes and speak with my hands. I'm fine just the way I am." Miranda lifted her chin and straightened her shoulders.

"You're better than fine," Boone signed, sticking his thumb in the center of his chest and wiggled his fingers.

A smile spread across Miranda's face. He meant it.

"I've got to get this boat back to Mr. Frechette." Boone tugged on the starter rope and the engine sputtered back to life in a cloud of yellowish-gray smoke. "I'll drop you off at the bluff and meet you later at your house, okay?"

Miranda nodded. She held her hand out for the

hearing aids.

"What are you going to do with them?" Boone asked.

Miranda did not reply. Maybe she shouldn't throw them away. But she wasn't going to take them home to Virginia with her.

"I already baked the cake," Aunt Kit said, dusting flour off her nose with a potholder. "It turned out all right. Just a little lopsided, that's all."

Miranda grinned. Aunt Kit's birthday cakes always suffered some calamity—they stuck in the pan, rose too high, or cracked down the middle. But it didn't matter. Today she was turning thirteen, and even a lopsided cake couldn't ruin that.

"I took a look at the garden wall," Aunt Kit said. "I don't believe it. It took the two of you all summer, but you did it. What with Boone's stay in the hospital, I thought the wall would never be finished." She gave Miranda a searching stare.

Miranda looked innocently back at her. She knew Aunt Kit still wondered what had really happened that night back in June.

Mr. Leach had been waiting for them at the edge of the beach as New Moon Island vanished in the sunrise.

"Thought you might be taking my yarns too serious," he said, wrapping them both in rough wool blankets and pouring a thermos full of hot sugary tea down their throats. "Can't have that on my conscience. You wouldn't be the first fools to turn up half-drowned on this particular stretch of beach when the moon's smiling."

Mr. Leach bundled the two of them in the cab of his truck and snuck Miranda back to her aunt's house before the sky grew light. Then he rousted Boone's mother, telling her as he rushed to the ferry that Boone had set out early to check lobster traps. "Must have slipped off the wharf and hit his head," Mr. Leach said.

It took the doctors in the hospital over at Rockland one full week to thaw the ice that seemed to flow through Boone's veins, a week to cure the pneumonia from the salt water that he had sucked into his lungs.

Miranda spent every daylight hour of that week working on the wall. She hauled and cleaned and lifted rocks until she was so tired that she couldn't think, so exhausted that she didn't miss the dreams that no longer prowled her sleep.

But she said nothing to Kit.

"You ready?" Kit asked, dropping a spoonful of maple frosting on top of the cake and spreading it with a broad knife. "Boone will be here soon."

Miranda smiled. Last year she and Timothy had carted hot dogs and marshmallows and sleeping bags out to the field to count shooting stars.

Her lip quivered.

This year she and Boone would camp out, and maybe it wouldn't be the best birthday ever. But it would be a good one.

Miranda flicked her index fingers away from

her and pointed to the staircase.

"When Boone gets here, I'll send him upstairs," Aunt Kit responded.

Miranda bounded up the steps two at a time and crossed the threshold to Timothy's room. She pulled the star guide down from the bookshelf over his desk, smoothing the cover flat with her hand. It was worn and creased, the corners dog-eared from much use.

She looked up and gazed around the room. The stand of birch trees outside, pale as smoke, cast their lengthening shadows through the window as the sun sank behind them. The air was still.

Miranda reached down in the pocket of her jeans and closed her hand around the meteorite, rubbing the glassy surface with her thumb.

She moved over to the window and searched the cobalt sky. A lone star glowed faintly orange in the dusk.

Pointing to her eyes, Miranda shaped two fingers into a V and swept them outward. Then she touched her fingers to her heart. "Look in," she signed.

She stood at the window, hand pressed against her chest, until Boone rode up on his bicycle, a sleeping bag strapped behind his seat. Seeing her, he smiled and waved.

She waved back.

Then folding the legs of the tripod carefully under the tube of the telescope, Miranda lifted it and went downstairs.